Dibble and Dabble

by Dave and Julie Saunders

Bradbury Press **New York**

It was a lovely summer's day. Dibble and Dabble, the two white ducks, were swimming in the river.

Suddenly in the reeds they saw something very strange.

It was a furry snake!

Dibble and Dabble were scared. They jumped into the water and swam up the river as fast as they could.

Under the bank they met Vole.

"What's the matter?" said Vole.

"We've seen a long furry snake in the reeds,

and we think he's coming!"

"Wait for me," called Vole.

Beside the lilypads they met Frog.

"What's going on?" said Frog.

"We've seen a scary long furry snake in the reeds,

and he's coming this way!"

"Wait for me," croaked Frog.

In the shady glade they met Fish.

"What's up?" said Fish.

"We've seen a horrible scary long furry snake

in the reeds, *and he's coming after us!*"

"Wait for me," said Fish.

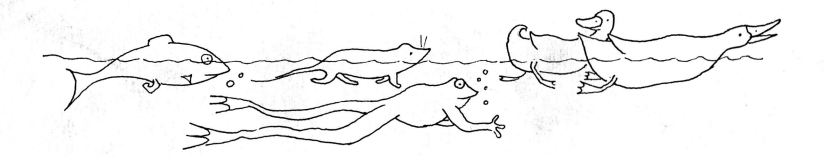

By the old tree stump they met Kingfisher.

"What's the rush?" said Kingfisher.

"We've seen a fat horrible scary long furry snake
in the reeds, *and he's coming closer!*"

"Wait for me," said Kingfisher.

In the shallow bay they met Heron.

"Where are you all going?" said Heron.

"We've seen an enormous fat horrible scary long furry snake in the reeds, *and he's close behind us!*"

"Wait for me," said Heron.

They met Pete in his boat.

"Steady on you lot," said Pete. "What's the matter?"

"We've seen a gigantic enormous fat horrible scary long furry snake in the reeds, *and he's chasing us!*"

"Follow me," said Pete. "We'll go and see."

Back downstream they all went, back to the reeds.

Pete stopped the boat and everyone gazed.

The furry snake moved and. . .

began to disappear and...

turned into Tigger the cat.

How they all laughed!

81219

E
S   Saunders, Dave
          Dibble and Dabble

        $13.95